Clarion Books
a Houghton Mifflin Company imprint
215 Park Avenue South, New York, NY 10003
Text and illustrations copyright © 2005 by Clavis Uitgeverij Amsterdam-Hasselt.
Translation copyright © 2006 by Houghton Mifflin Company.

First published as *Benno is nooit bang* in Amsterdam-Hasselt in 2005
by Clavis Uitgeverij. First American edition, 2006.

The illustrations were executed in oils.
The text was set in 22-point LT Tapeside.

www.houghtonmifflinbooks.com

Printed in Italy.

Library of Congress Cataloging-in-Publication Data

Robberecht, Thierry.
[Benno is nooit bang. English]
Sam is never scared / by Thierry Robberecht ; illustrated by Philippe Goossens.—1st American ed.
p. cm.
Summary: Sam feels fearless compared to Max, who is afraid of climbing trees and watching scary movies,
until Sam learns that everyone is afraid of something.
ISBN-13: 978-0-618-73278-4
ISBN-10: 0-618-73278-0
[1. Fear—Fiction.] I. Goossens, Philippe, ill. II. Title.
PZ7.R53233Sam 2005
[E]—dc22
2005031750

10 9 8 7 6 5 4 3 2 1

Sam Is NEVER Scared

by Thierry Robberecht

Illustrated by Philippe Goossens

Clarion Books
New York

I'm Sam.

And I'm not scared of anything.

At least, that's what all my friends think.

At the playground, I'm the only one

who goes down the slide headfirst.

My friend Max is afraid of everything.
He won't even stand on the swings.
"You're such a scaredy-cat, Max!" I say.

9

When we watch scary movies,
Max closes his eyes during all the good parts.

But the truth is that sometimes I DO get scared.
At night, when there might be monsters
under my bed or ghosts behind my curtains.
But I would never tell my friends that.

One day I wanted to teach Max how to climb a tree.

But he was too scared to even try.

We had to play boring soccer instead.

While we were playing,

I found a spider on my hand.

A gigantic hairy spider with extra-long legs!

I was so scared, I couldn't even move.

Then I started to cry.

But Max just picked up the spider
and placed it on a leaf.
He may be afraid of a lot of things,
but he isn't afraid of spiders.
"Thanks, Max," I said. "That was really brave."

That night I was more scared than ever.
Not of the monsters under my bed
or the ghosts behind my curtains.
I was scared of Max.
What if he told everyone I cried?
I could already hear them calling me
"Scaredy-cat Sam."

21

When my dad came in to say good night,
I told him what happened.
"Everyone is scared of something," he said.
"Even you?" I asked.

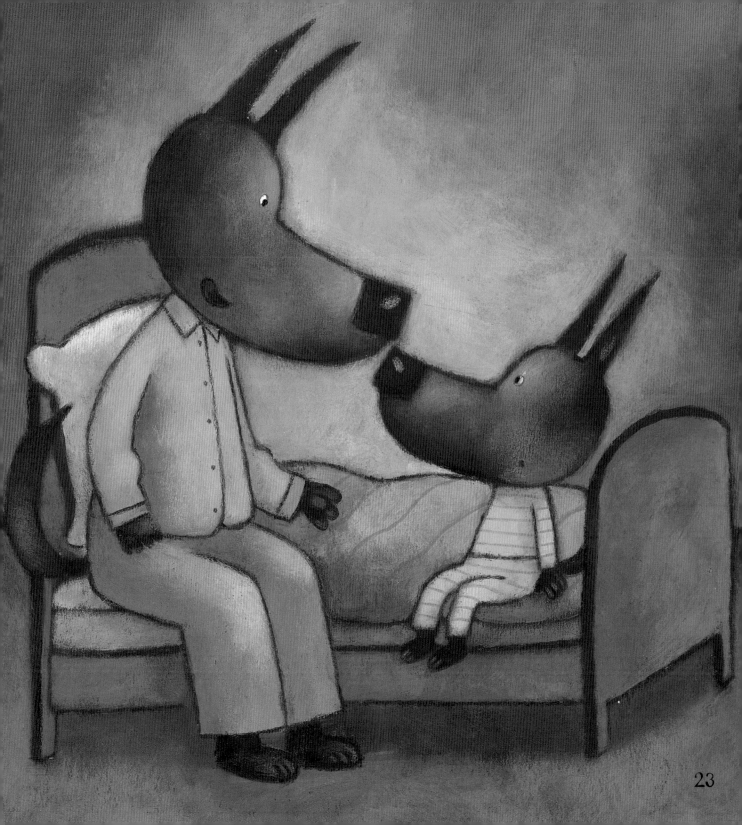

"Even me," said Dad.

"When I was your age, I used to be afraid
of monsters and ghosts."

"Me, too!" I said.

So together we searched under my bed
and behind my curtains.

But all we found was my missing dinosaur.

25

Max never told anyone about the spider.

And he seemed different after that.

One day he even went down the slide headfirst!

I'm different, too.

I'm still Sam.

But now I'm really not scared of anything.

Not even of being a scaredy-cat.